Getting Children Started with Books

On more than one occasion you've probably found yourself having to choose a book for a young child. As you faced an entire rack or shelf of children's books and wondered which one to select, you probably asked yourself: Which book will be appealing? Is it the appropriate reading level?

The book that you have in your hand right now is suited to children who are ages six to nine. Yearling books can be read aloud to children or they can be read independently by those children who are reading on their own.

After a child has read this book alone or with an adult, that child is ready for the suggested activities which follow. These activities follow directly from the story and provide the child with opportunities to think, to explore, and to have fun.

FUN TO **READ**

FUN TO DO!

After you've read
**CAM JANSEN AND THE MYSTERY OF
THE DINOSAUR BONES**
here are some activities you might want to try:

1. Cam has a rather amazing mental camera. Though you may not have a photographic memory like Cam's, you can use your memory to learn a new song or poem. After you have memorized something, share it with a friend.

2. Make a list of all the clues that Cam and her friend Eric uncover as they solve the mystery of the dinosaur bones.

3. Cam knew about the Coelophysis because she had read about it. What dinosaur have you read about? Stegosaurus? Brontosaurus? Pterodactyl? Tyrannosaurus rex? Triceratops? Read about a dinosaur that is new to you, then tell a grown-up what you've learned.

4. Ask an older brother, sister, or an adult to help you make models of your handprint or footprint. Mix plaster of paris with water. Pour the plaster into an aluminum pie pan and let it harden slightly. Carefully place your hand (or foot) into the mixture. When the plaster hardens, your print will be visible.

CAM JANSEN

and the
Mystery of the
Dinosaur Bones

DAVID A. ADLER
Illustrated by Susanna Natti

A Yearling Book

Published by
Dell Publishing
a division of
The Bantam Doubleday Dell Publishing Group, Inc.
666 Fifth Avenue
New York, New York 10103

ISBN: 0-440-41199-8

Reprinted by arrangement with The Viking Press

Printed in the United States of America

January 1983

10 9

To two wonderful people,
my parents

Chapter One

"*Slurp.*"

Cam Jansen was drinking milk through a straw. She tilted the container to get the last few drops.

Cam was eating lunch in the cafeteria of the Kurt Daub Museum. She was there with her fifth-grade class. Her friend Eric Shelton was sitting next to her.

Cam pointed to the teacher. The teacher was standing on a chair with a finger over her mouth.

"Look," Cam said to Eric. "Ms. Benson is waiting for us to be quiet."

"Our tour will begin in twenty minutes," Ms. Benson said. "But first I must ask those of you who brought cameras along to keep your cameras in their cases. The

taking of photographs in the museum is not allowed."

Ms. Benson got down from the chair.

"See," Cam said to Eric, "I told you not to bring your camera. Last time I was here someone was told to leave the museum because he was taking pictures."

"Well," Eric said, "maybe I can't take pictures, but you can. Take a picture of me now with your mental camera."

Cam's mental camera is her memory. She can take one look at a page in a book, close her eyes, and remember every word on the page. "It's easy for me," Cam often explained. "I have a photograph of the page stored in my brain. When I want to remember what I saw, I just look at the photograph."

When people found out about Cam's amazing photographic memory, they stopped using her real name, Jennifer. They started calling her "The Camera."

Soon "The Camera" was shortened to "Cam."

Cam looked straight at Eric and said, *"Click."* She always said, *"Click,"* when she wanted to remember something. Cam says that *"Click"* is the sound her mental camera makes when it takes a picture.

"Close your eyes," Eric said. "Now what do you remember?"

Cam thought for a moment. Then she said, "There's a drop of mustard on your collar. You should wipe it off!"

Eric looked down. There *was* a drop of mustard on his collar. He took a napkin and wiped it off.

"On the side of the milk container you just bought," Cam went on, "it says, 'Edna's. Our cows send you their love and their milk.'

"You're wearing a blue shirt. The top button of the shirt once came off and someone sewed it back on."

4

"You're right," Eric said. "But how did you know about the button?"

Cam opened her eyes. "It's the thread," she said. "I remembered that the top button was sewn on with white thread. The other buttons have light blue thread."

Ms. Benson was standing on a chair again. She said to the class, "Clean your tables and then get into a double line."

Cam and Eric quickly threw away the empty milk containers and the wrappings from their lunches. Then they got in line.

Ms. Benson led the class up the stairs to the museum lobby. They were met there by a young woman in a purple dress.

"I'm Janet Tyler," the woman in the purple dress said. "I will be your guide. Please stay together and follow me."

The guide led the class to the Air Travel room. She pointed out the models of the earliest flying machines. There was a full-size model of the 1903 Wright brothers' airplane.

Ms. Tyler took the class to a weather station room with a solar energy exhibit. Then she led the class into a large room with a very high ceiling.

"This next exhibit is my favorite," the guide told the class.

"Mine, too," Cam whispered to Eric.

Chapter Two

The class followed the guide into the room. Glass cases filled with old tools, bones, rocks, and photographs lined the walls. On a platform, in the center of the room, was part of the skeleton of a very large dinosaur, the Brachiosaurus. Some of the bones from the skeleton were lying on the platform. The wires had come loose and the skeleton was being repaired.

"This is the skeleton of a Brachiosaurus. Brake-e-o-sawr-us," Janet Tyler said again slowly so everyone could hear how the word was pronounced. "The Brachiosaurus was the biggest dinosaur. It weighed over fifty tons. That's more, I'm sure, than all the children in your whole school weigh together."

Then the guide led the class to another dinosaur skeleton. It was much smaller than the Brachiosaurus. Its mouth was open and its hands were stretched out as if it were ready to grab something to eat.

"Look at those teeth," someone in the class said.

"And look at that tail. It's so long and pointy."

"This is the skeleton of a Coelophysis," the guide said. "Seel-o-fy-sis," she said again slowly. "Now you may know about some dinosaurs, but I'm sure no one knows anything about the Coelophysis."

"I do," Cam said.

Everyone turned to look at Cam. They were surprised that she knew about the

Coelophysis. Ms. Benson had never mentioned it when she taught the class about dinosaurs.

Cam had read about the Coelophysis. She wanted to remember exactly what the book said. She closed her eyes and said, *"Click."*

When Cam said, *"Click,"* the guide started to laugh. She covered her mouth with her hand.

"The Coelophysis," Cam said with her eyes still closed, "was one of the first dinosaurs. It was about eight feet long, including its tail. It weighed no more than fifty pounds. It was a meat eater and . . ."

"Yes, thank you," the guide said before Cam had a chance to finish. "What you may not know is that these bones were discovered by Dr. Kurt Daub, the scientist who started this museum."

"Are people still finding dinosaur bones?" Eric asked.

"Yes," Ms. Tyler answered. "I'll be going on a dinosaur hunt in a few weeks, and I hope to find some myself."

Someone else asked, "Are all those bones real?"

"No. Dr. Daub didn't find a complete skeleton. Some of these bones were made from plaster of Paris."

There were many other questions, but Cam stopped listening. She was busy studying the dinosaur's tail.

"Something is wrong," she whispered to Eric.

Cam closed her eyes and said, *"Click."* She kept them closed for a while. Then she

looked again at the dinosaur's tail.

"I was right," Cam said to Eric. "Something *is* wrong. Three of the dinosaur's bones are missing."

Chapter Three

Cam raised her hand and tried to get the museum guide's attention. But Ms. Tyler looked past her.

The guide pointed to a boy wearing a suit and a bow tie. "You have a question."

"I want to know why they are called dinosaurs."

Ms. Tyler smiled. "The name 'dinosaur' comes from two words, 'dino' which means 'terrible,' and 'saur' which means 'lizard.' So when we call them dinosaurs, we are really calling them terrible lizards."

"What did dinosaurs eat?" another boy asked.

"Some ate meat. Some ate plants, and some ate the eggs of other dinosaurs."

Then the guide looked at Cam. She smiled. "It seems that the red-haired girl, the one who says, *'Click,'* has a question."

"What happened to the tail?" Cam asked. "The last time I was here, it had three more bones. They were right here."

Cam pointed to the part of the tail near the hip. Farther down, there were bones that hung down from the tail like ribs. Where Cam pointed there weren't any bones.

"There's nothing missing on this dinosaur," the guide said quickly. "Now, are there any other questions?"

"But there *are* some bones missing. I've been here before and—"

"I'm here every day, and this skeleton

16

looks the same as it always does."

The guide answered a few other questions. Then she told Ms. Benson that the tour was finished, and she walked away.

Ms. Benson was a short woman. She stood on her toes so the whole class could see her.

"It's still early," Ms. Benson said. "You

have an hour to go through the museum by yourselves. At two-thirty all of you must be in the front lobby. If you don't have a watch, please stay near someone who does."

"Let's go to the gift shop," Eric said to Cam. "I want to buy presents for my twin sisters and my brother, Howie."

In the gift shop there were shelves of books and racks of postcards. Kits to make airplane models and models of dinosaurs were piled on a table with toys and games.

"All I have is a dollar," Eric said. "I hope I can find something."

While Eric looked around, Cam opened a big book called *Dinosaurs*. There was a whole page on the Coelophysis, but there was no illustration of its skeleton. The book told about how the Coelophysis hunted for food and how it might have looked, but it did not say how many bones the Coelophysis had in its tail.

"Look what I bought for the twins," Eric said a few minutes later. He reached into a bag and took out two small whistles, each in the shape of a Brachiosaurus. Cam took one of the whistles and blew into it. It was a dog whistle. It made a sound dogs could hear clearly, but Cam and Eric could hardly hear it.

"These whistles are for calling dogs," Cam said. "Why did you buy them? Your family doesn't have a dog."

"I know, but these whistles are also toy dinosaurs, and they're just twenty-nine cents each. Everything else costs too much."

Eric reached into the bag again and took out two postcards. "Look at these," he said. "This one is for Howie." It was a picture of a hot-air balloon. "And this one is for me." The second postcard had a picture of the Coelophysis skeleton.

"Let me see that," Cam said.

Cam looked at the postcard carefully. Then she closed her eyes and said, *"Click."*

"This is it!" she said, waving the post-card. "This is the way the skeleton looked when I saw it the last time I was here. Let's go to the dinosaur room. You'll see. Some bones are missing."

Cam and Eric quickly walked through the museum.

"All right," Cam said when they stood in front of the Coelophysis skeleton. "You count the bones hanging from the tail of the skeleton. I'll count the ones on the postcard."

Cam counted the bones on the postcard a few times. Then she said, "I counted thirty-four on the tail. How many did you count?"

"Thirty-one."

Chapter Four

Cam looked at her watch. It was two-thirty.

"Come on, Eric," she said. "It's time to go."

Eric put the postcards and whistles in his pocket, and they went to meet the class in the lobby. Ms. Benson asked the class to line up. Then she led them to the school bus.

On the bus Cam and Eric talked about the missing dinosaur bones.

"Why would anyone want them?" Eric asked.

"And how could anyone steal the bones?" Cam added. "The skeleton is wired together. In the time it would take to unhook a bone, I'm sure someone would walk by and see what they were doing."

The bus stopped in the school parking lot. Ms. Benson stood up.

"It's after three o'clock," she said. "So you may all go home."

It was a warm spring day. Cam and Eric had ridden their bicycles to school that morning. They went to the rack behind the school to get their bicycles.

As Cam unlocked her bicycle, she said, "The bones can't be taken when the museum is open. There are too many people around then, and too many guards. It must be done after the museum closes. Let's go back there. Maybe we can find out what's going on."

"But the museum closes early today," Eric said. "We won't have any time to look around."

Cam put rubber bands over the cuffs of her pants to keep them from getting caught in the bicycle as she rode.

"All we have to look for is a place to hide," Cam said. "We don't have to be home until six today. We can stay in the dinosaur room after the museum closes and watch to see what happens."

Cam was already on her bicycle. She started to ride away before Eric could tell her that he didn't want to hide in the museum.

Eric got on his bicycle. He pedaled hard, but he couldn't catch up with Cam. By the time he locked his bicycle in front of the museum, Cam was halfway up the steps. He caught up with her in the dinosaur room.

A bell sounded.

"The museum closes in five minutes," a guard called out.

"Let's leave now," Eric said, "or we'll be locked inside."

Cam crawled under a glass case filled with photographs. Eric followed her.

Cam whispered to Eric, "You can leave if you want to, but I'm staying."

The bell sounded again.

From their hiding place Cam and Eric could see only the bottoms of the other exhibit cases and the feet of the dinosaur skeletons. A few people walked past the glass case, but all Cam and Eric could see were their legs. Then it was quiet.

"We did it," Cam said.

It was quiet for a while. But soon Cam and Eric heard footsteps. A man was walking from one case to the next. He stopped at Cam and Eric's case. Then he bent down and looked straight at Cam and Eric.

Chapter Five

It was one of the museum guards.

"Come with me," he said.

The guard led them out of the dinosaur room, through the museum lobby, to the office of the museum director. The guard knocked on the door and walked in. Cam and Eric followed him.

The walls of the office were covered with paintings of prehistoric animals. There were statues of famous scientists and large stuffed animals all over the room. Cam and

Eric couldn't find the director among all those paintings and statues.

"Didn't you hear the bell?" the director asked.

Then Cam and Eric saw him. He was sitting between a statue of a woman scientist and two stuffed owls.

"Yes, we heard the bell," Cam said. "But three dinosaur bones are missing. Someone is stealing bones from the tail of the Coelophysis skeleton, and we want to see who it is."

"That's impossible," the director said, stroking his beard. "Nothing is missing. But if you want to watch over the Coelophysis, you can come back tomorrow when the museum opens." Then he said to the guard, "Now please take these children to the door and make sure that this time they leave the museum."

Cam and Eric followed the guard to the front entrance. The guard opened the door with a key and let them out.

"Now what?" Eric asked.

"There's nothing we can do," Cam said. "We can't get back inside, so let's go home."

While Cam and Eric started to unlock their bicycles, a truck rode past them. It backed into the museum driveway. A sign painted on the side of the truck said, "Beth's Milk Tastes Best."

"That's strange," Cam said. "Milk is usually delivered early in the morning, not late in the afternoon."

A man in a white uniform got out of the truck. He was carrying an empty milk box.

"Maybe some of the milk went bad," Eric said, "and he's picking it up."

The milkman knocked on the garage door. The door opened and he went inside. He came out a few minutes later, carrying a large brown bag in the box. He put it in the truck.

"There's probably a whole bunch of containers of sour milk in that bag," Eric said.

Cam and Eric heard the door on the other side of the truck open and someone get inside, but they couldn't see who it was. Then the truck backed up. As the truck passed them, Cam read the sign again.

"There's something else that's strange about that truck," Cam said. She closed her eyes and said, *"Click."*

"The museum doesn't use Beth's milk. It uses Edna's. That's what it said on the milk container you bought in the cafeteria."

Cam got on her bicycle. She turned to Eric and said, "That man wasn't picking up sour milk. He was picking up something else. Come on, let's follow the truck."

Chapter Six

The streets were crowded with cars. It was after four o'clock, and many people were driving home from work. Cam stayed on the right-hand side of the street. Eric rode behind her. The milk truck was already a block ahead. Cam and Eric pedaled hard to catch up.

As Cam pedaled, her bicycle made a loud "clicking" sound. The kickstand was loose, and one of the pedals hit it as it went around.

The milk truck made a right turn onto a

side street, but before Cam and Eric could reach the corner, Cam had to stop. The loose kickstand was in the way. It was impossible for Cam to pedal.

Eric got off his bicycle, too. He pushed the kickstand on Cam's bicycle back into place.

Cam said, "Thank you."

"You really need a new one," Eric told her.

Cam and Eric got on their bicycles again. When they reached the corner, they signaled and turned.

Cam looked ahead. A big brown dog was running along the sidewalk. A few cars were parked along the side of the street. But Cam couldn't see the milk truck. She stopped and waited for Eric.

"We've lost it," Cam said.

"Maybe not. I think I see a truck parked in the driveway of one of the houses on the next block. Maybe it's the milk truck."

Eric led Cam to a small brick house with a white wooden fence around it. The milk truck was parked in the driveway. No one was sitting inside the truck.

"They must have gone into the house," Cam said. She leaned her bicycle against the fence. "You stay here and watch for them," she told Eric. "I'll look around in the back."

There was a high window on the side of the garage. As Cam walked past the window, she heard voices. She looked for something to stand on so she could see inside.

Someone tapped her on the back. It was Eric.

"I locked the bicycles to the fence," he said. "I didn't want to wait out there alone."

Cam found an empty wooden milk box behind the house. She put the box right under the window, climbed up, and looked through.

There was a large table inside the garage. A few small bones and some larger ones were on the table. The milk box with the brown bag that they had seen the man put in the truck was there, too. A bag of plaster of Paris was on the floor near some boxes, and metal tubs and a wheelbarrow with a pickax and shovel in it.

"Get down," Eric whispered. "Someone will see you."

"There's no one there," Cam said. "But there is an open door. Maybe it leads into the house. I'll bet that's where they went."

Eric climbed up on the box.

"Look!" Eric said. "The three missing bones are on that table!"

Eric got off the box. He pulled on Cam's sleeve. "Get down," he said. "Let's go back now."

Cam didn't move. She kept looking through the window.

"We can call the museum," Eric said. "We can tell them we found their missing dinosaur bones."

"Someone is coming through the door," Cam said. "It's the Milkman."

Eric quickly climbed onto the box. Cam

and Eric watched the Milkman take the brown bag out of the box. The bag was tied with string. The Milkman tried to untie the knot. He couldn't.

"Why did you tie it so tight?" he called into the house.

"Use the scissors," a woman's voice answered.

The Milkman reached into one of the boxes. He took out a pair of scissors and cut the string.

"I wonder what could be in there," Eric whispered.

"It can't be a bone from the Coelophysis," Cam said quietly. "It's too big."

The Milkman tore open the side of the bag. There was something large and white inside. He took it out and carefully placed it on the table.

"Wow!" Eric said. "Look at the size of that bone."

"It must be from the Brachiosaurus,"

Cam said, "the one they were fixing in the museum."

The Milkman took out a ruler and measured the bone. He took a pad and pencil from his pocket and wrote on the pad. Then he looked at the bag of plaster of Paris.

"We need more plaster," he called into the house.

"Then let's go get it," the woman said. The Milkman walked through the open door and into the house.

"They'll probably use the plaster of Paris to make a copy of the bone," Cam said. "They'll take the copy to the museum tomorrow and leave it there in place of the real one."

"But how do they get in and out of the museum?" Eric asked.

"And why do they want the bones?" Cam added.

Cam and Eric stopped talking. They heard the front door of the house open and then slam shut.

After a few minutes Cam whispered, "I didn't hear the truck drive away, but they should be gone by now. Let's take a look."

Cam walked quietly. Eric followed her. Cam peeked out past the edge of the garage wall. She saw that the truck was still in the driveway. And she saw something else.

"Our bicycles," Cam said. "What if *they* see them!"

Chapter Seven

"We sure did see your bicycles," a man said.

Cam turned. It was the Milkman. He was standing behind Eric.

"Janet!" the Milkman called.

A woman came out. She was wearing a purple dress. It was Janet Tyler, the museum guide.

"Well, well," she said. "Look who we have here. It's the Click, Click Girl and her friend."

The Milkman put a key into a lock at the side of the garage door. The lock was electric. He turned the key and the door opened.

The Milkman led Cam and Eric into the garage. He pressed a button on the wall. The garage door closed.

Janet Tyler and the Milkman started to argue. She pointed to the dinosaur bones on the table.

"It's all over. We'll have to give these back. And it's your fault. You should have made copies of the three small bones last night. Then these kids wouldn't have followed us."

"I'm not giving anything back. Not yet," the Milkman said. "We'll do just as we planned. We'll take the bones along on our dinosaur hunt. We'll bury them and then dig them up. *Then* we'll give the bones back to the museum."

Janet closed her eyes and said, "I can just see the newspaper headline: 'Janet Tyler discovers buried dinosaur bones and gives them to the museum.' I'll be famous. I'll speak to science groups all over the country. I'll make a fortune."

Cam pulled on Eric's sleeve and whispered, "This is our chance. Janet's eyes are closed. Take out the whistles you bought."

Eric reached into his pocket. He took out the two dog whistles shaped like dinosaurs. Cam took one of them.

"When I tell you to, blow the whistle," Cam whispered. "Blow it as hard as you can."

"Stop whispering," the Milkman said.

Janet opened her eyes. She seemed surprised to be in the garage with Cam, Eric, and the Milkman.

Then the Milkman told Cam and Eric, "Either you agree not to tell anyone about our plan, or we'll call the museum director. We'll put the bones in your bicycle baskets and tell the director you took them and we caught you."

44

Cam turned to whisper to Eric.

Janet Tyler smiled. "That's right," she said. "You talk it over with your friend."

"Quietly count to three," Cam whispered. "Then blow the whistle."

"One. . ."

Cam quickly turned around. She pressed the garage door button.

"Two. . ."

The garage door opened.

"Three."

Cam and Eric blew the whistles hard.

Janet could hardly hear the sounds the whistles made. But she knew what kind of whistles they were.

"Get the bones!" Janet yelled. "Get the bones before some dog comes and runs off with them."

She opened the door to the house. The Milkman picked up as many of the bones as he could carry.

"Quick, Eric!" Cam said. "Crawl under the table."

Chapter Eight

Cam and Eric crawled under the table and ran out of the garage. A big brown dog and two smaller dogs ran past them toward the garage.

Cam and Eric ran around the milk truck to the bicycles. Eric tried to open the lock. He turned the dial a few times.

"Hurry!" Cam said.

"I can't remember the combination."

Cam closed her eyes. She said, *"Click."* Then she thought for a moment.

Inside the house there was a noise. Someone was coming out.

"It's four, eighteen, thirty-six," Cam said.

Eric turned the knob. The lock opened. Cam and Eric got on their bicycles just as the Milkman ran out of the house.

"Stop!" he yelled.

"Let's go!" Cam said to Eric.

Cam looked both ways. No cars were coming. She quickly rode across the street. Eric followed her.

Just as they got across the street, they heard the door of the milk truck open and shut. The engine started.

Cam pedaled hard. As she pedaled, her bicycle made a loud clicking sound. She tried to keep pedaling, but she couldn't. The kickstand was in the way.

Cam got off her bicycle. Eric stopped, too. He came over to help.

"Hurry. The truck's coming," Cam said.

Eric pushed the kickstand back into place. They both got back on their bicycles.

Cam started pedaling again. The bicycle made a clicking sound, but not as loud as before.

Cam turned quickly and looked behind

her. Eric was pedaling hard. And the milk truck was right behind Eric.

Cam pedaled as hard as she could. The clicking sound became louder again, but Cam kept pedaling. She signaled and turned the corner. Eric followed her.

"*Screech!*"

"*Honk! Honk!*"

Cam stopped pedaling and turned to see what was happening. A car had turned the corner right in front of the milk truck. Both the driver of the car and the Milkman had slammed on their brakes.

"This is our chance," Cam told Eric.

Cam and Eric were riding on a busy street now. There were stores on both sides of the street.

Cam saw a narrow path on the side of a candy store. She rode down the path to the back of the store. Eric followed her.

"Good thinking," Eric said once they had stopped their bicycles. "When the Milkman turns the corner, he won't be able to find us."

Cam got off her bicycle. Then she told Eric, "You stay here and watch the bikes. I'm going inside to call the museum."

There was only one telephone in the store. A large man was using it. Cam opened the telephone book and looked for the museum's number.

"Do you have any shirts on sale?" the man was saying into the telephone. "Yes . . . Extra-large . . . I want a sky-blue shirt. But not a rainy day sky-blue. It should be a sunny day sky-blue."

Cam found the museum's number. She looked at it and said, *"Click."* Then she took a coin from her pocket and waited to use the phone.

". . . and I need a green shirt," the man said into the telephone. "But not grass-green. It should be more like a traffic-light green . . ."

Eric came into the store. "I saw the milk truck. It rode right past me. The Milkman and Janet Tyler looked angry, but they didn't see me or the bicycles."

The man said, "Thank you very much." He hung up and left the booth.

Cam said, *"Click,"* to help her remember the museum's number. Then she dialed.

"Hello," Cam said into the telephone. "I'd like to speak to the director."

She waited.

"This is Jennifer Jansen," Cam said. "I'm the girl who was found hiding in the dinosaur room after the museum closed."

Cam told the director about the Milkman, Janet Tyler, and the dinosaur bones. She also told him the name and address of the candy store. "Yes, we'll wait here for you," Cam said, and then she hung up.

"The museum director is coming," Cam told Eric. "He said that after we left, he went to the dinosaur room. He looked at the skeletons and saw that some bones were missing. He said we should wait in front of the store with our bicycles. When he gets here, he'll follow us to the house."

Chapter Nine

Cam and Eric went behind the store to get their bicycles. Eric started turning the dial on the lock.

"Do you remember the combination?" Cam asked.

"Sure, I only forgot the last time because we were in such a hurry."

As Eric was turning the dial, Cam laughed and said, "You know, I don't think any dog would really be interested in those dinosaur bones. They're too old."

Cam and Eric walked their bicycles to the

front of the candy store. They waited for the museum director.

Soon a car drove up and stopped in front of the store. The car was just like the museum exhibits—very old. The director was at the wheel. He waved to Cam and Eric. They got on their bicycles. The director followed them in his car to the small brick house with the white wooden fence. The milk truck was in the driveway again.

"This is it," Cam told the director.

"You don't have to worry about the bones," the director said. "Since I know Janet stole them, she can't bury the bones and pretend to discover them. The bones are no good to her any more, so I'm sure she'll give them back without any trouble."

The museum director got out of his car. "Of course, she'll lose her job and I'll have to report her and her friend to the police. But they should have known that could happen when they took the bones."

The museum director shook hands with Cam and Eric. "I want to thank both of you for all your help," he said. "Before you go, you must tell me how you knew that some bones were missing. I pass those skeletons all the time, and I didn't notice anything."

Cam explained, "The last time I was at the museum, I took a picture of the dinosaur skeleton. When I looked at the picture, I knew some bones were missing."

"But our guards don't let anyone take photographs in the museum."

"Cam's camera is different," said Eric. "She doesn't need film or a flash. Cam's camera is her memory."

The director smiled. "Well, we certainly won't stop your memory from taking photographs." He buttoned his jacket, and then he asked, "Can you take one of me?"

Cam laughed. Then she looked straight at the museum director and said, *"Click."*